Miranda the Great

Miranda the Great

Eleanor Estes

With illustrations by Edward Ardizzone

AN ODYSSEY/HARCOURT YOUNG CLASSIC

HARCOURT, INC.

Orlando   Austin   New York   San Diego   Toronto   London

To Ruth

www.HarcourtBooks.com

First Harcourt Young Classics edition 2005
First Odyssey Classics edition 2005
First published 1967

Library of Congress Cataloging-in-Publication Data
Estes, Eleanor, 1906–1988.
Miranda the Great/by Eleanor Estes; illustrated by Edward Ardizzone.
p. cm.
Summary: When barbarians invade ancient Rome
and Miranda the cat is separated from her owners, she and her
daughter lead a group of kittens to safety in the Coliseum.
[1. Cats—Fiction. 2. Heroes—Fiction. 3. Mothers—Fiction.
4. Rome—History—Fiction.] I. Ardizzone, Edward, 1900– ill. II. Title.
PZ7.E749Mir   2005
[Fic]—dc22   2004042364
ISBN-13: 978-0152-05405-2   ISBN-10: 0-15-205405-7
ISBN-13: 978-0152-05411-3 (pb)   ISBN-10: 0-15-205411-1 (pb)

Printed in the United States of America

A C E G H F D B
A C E G H F D B (pb)

CONTENTS

Miranda

In Rome, long, long ago, there lived a gold-colored cat named Miranda. She was two and one half years old, and so far she had had two sets of kittens. Her silvery gray daughter, Punka, one of her first kittens and her favorite, lived with her still. Up to now, Miranda's life had been happy and calm, chasing butterflies, bees, and little yellow birds, watching her reflection in the pool, waiting patiently for a raindrop to fall from a leaf, and minding her kittens, for she was a good mother.

Miranda was a good singer, too, and often sang in the nighttime of these happy days. She lived with a little girl named Claudia, who was seven. Claudia had had Miranda since she was a tiny kitten and had watched her grow, holding her in her lap and giving her drops of goat's milk to make her big and strong. This did make Miranda big and strong, and her kittens had all been big and strong also.

Claudia's friends called Miranda and Punka "giant cats." "Why, they are colossal!" they exclaimed. Punka, though more than a year younger, was even larger than her mother.

"She is the little one!" Claudia would say, delighting in her friends' confusion.

"Little!" they would say. "Why, she is colossal, too!"

Claudia and her family lived in a pretty golden marble house, not far from the Colosseum in Rome. Claudia's mother was named Lavinia, and sometimes she played the lyre. Both cats loved music. Punka would roll over on her back and blissfully close her eyes and purr when Lavinia played. Once she had plucked a string of the lyre herself and made a sound, which proved how musical she was. However, she could not sing. "Wah!" was her only note. A bee had once stung Punka on her nose and on her throat, and this had ruined her singing forevermore, giving her voice its gritty sound.

Claudia's father, Marcus, was a senator in the Roman Forum. Before this, he had been a mighty soldier in the army and had fought in Spain. It was there that Marcus had found Zag, their great and wise dog. He had rescued the tiny, trembling brown-and-white puppy, a spaniel, from the fierce cats of Barcelona and had carried her, held snugly under his tunic, across the Pyrenees and across the plains and all the way home to Rome.

Naturally, for Zag, the world revolved around her rescuer, Marcus. When Marcus was at the Senate, Zag lay gloomily at the garden gate, her head pointing toward the Forum, her mouth in a mournful droop while she waited for him to come back. Miranda sometimes washed Zag's face to cheer her up. Zag's groans as she endured this motherly attention were varied and expressive and had earned her the nickname, "the talking dog." She talked also when she wanted some of the food the others were eating. She talked to Marcus, reproaching him for being late, when at last he would come home, fling off his toga, stomp around the garden pool, and exclaim, "'They're coming!' I say to them in the Senate. 'I've said it before, and I say it again! The barbarians are coming! Get ready! Go forth and stop the hordes,' I say, 'or they will sack the city,' I say. 'Rome!' Do they heed me? No! They do not. They flock to the Colosseum instead to watch the games . . . ts!" Marcus would shout, and he would fling himself into the pool and have a good splashing swim.

Miranda and Punka always raced to the flower garden, shaking their heads as though they had gotten a drop of water on them, and hid from the noisy man. But Zag would join her master in the bath, try to lick his face and his beard, swim with him, and catch a ball.

Then, shivering happily, Zag would shake herself and lie in the sun near the garden wall under a pretty tile mosaic that had a picture of a fierce dog on it and the words, "*Cave canem.*"

Beware the dog! Marcus had put this tile in the garden wall as a joke, for Zag had never bitten anybody. She never even chased cats.

Miranda had to do it all, chase dogs, chase cats, be the brave one, mind Punka, mind Zag.

Once last winter, after a terrible and unusual snowstorm, Miranda had chased sixteen dogs off their street. They were trotting along happily through the deep and snowy ravine in the middle of the street where men and animals had worn a path. Suddenly Miranda had leaped into the ravine and chased the sixteen dogs away. None of them had the courage to turn around and fight the fierce and terrible cat. Their flight

was a disgrace to the dogs of Rome and one of the first of Miranda's great triumphs.

"You are a great cat," Zag had said to her admiringly.

"Oh-woe," said Miranda modestly.

And no cat was allowed on her street either. The cats of Rome knew this by now. However, there had been one cat who came in the night. This was the great and awful lizard cat with the broken tail who had come from Barcelona in Spain to Rome. He had been driven out of

Barcelona by the terrible rooftop cats there because of his tyrannical ways. He had made his own way over the high Pyrenees, not snuggled up closely to some warm human under a warm toga as Zag had been. But by himself, all by himself, he had come to Rome, and he sang in the nighttime of his wanderings. Sometimes Miranda joined in the singing, and these duets were her first great singing. However, she told him he must stay off her street, to come no nearer than the high wall at the end of the alleyway behind their house and to sing there.

All cats minded Miranda and did what she said.

Flight

Today was Punka's birthday. She was one year old. Claudia had given her a dish of cream to celebrate, and now Miranda was washing her face. Miranda was telling Punka that she was going to have some more kittens soon, any day now. She purred happily and Punka purred, too. Punka promised to mind them sometimes so that Miranda could have some free time and keep the cats and dogs chased away.

All was peaceful in the garden. Claudia was writing her lessons on her tablet, learning the rules of the ablative absolute. Zag was lying at the garden gate waiting for Marcus. Lavinia was playing the lyre. Both cats rolled over on their backs, closed their eyes, and listened blissfully to the music.

Suddenly Miranda turned over. She sat up, turned her ears back, and narrowed her eyes. She scanned the sky. She began to clean one of her back legs, the better to think. Between licks, holding her leg stiff and stationary and ready for the next lick, she carefully sniffed the sunny air. She fastened her unblinking glass-green eyes on something she saw high up in the air...a cloud? Smoke?

Miranda closed her eyes, the better to smell. She drew in deep sniffs and with each sniff gave a little nod. She did smell smoke! Punka, because of the old bee-bite, smelled nothing. Anyway, she was used to having her mother tell her all the news, what to watch out for, what dog might be coming into their alleyway, and she did little thinking for herself. She continued to listen in ecstasy to the plucking of the strings of the lyre.

Zag had not smelled anything either. Her

nose had never been very good because of the mean cats of Barcelona. That made two pets in one family that had poor noses, and it was lucky that Miranda's was so excellent. Miranda went over to Zag and told her that she smelled smoke. "You must warn the people," Miranda told her. "Say, 'Ai-ooo! Ai-ooo! Smoke! Fire!'" Zag was a brilliant dog, but she did not smell the smoke, and so she was not going to say, "Ai-ooo!"

Then a cinder flew into Claudia's eye. She dropped her tablet and leaped up. "Mother!" she cried. "I smell smoke!"

Her mother quickly laid aside her lyre. "You are right, Claudia," she said. "I smell it, too."

At this moment Marcus raced up in his chariot. His toga was awry. He was covered with ashes. His horse, Hamilcar Barca, was neighing in terror. "Wuh-huh-huh-huh!" he said. "Wuh-huh-huh-huh!"

"Come!" shouted Marcus. "Rome is burning. The barbarians are sacking the city. The wind is rising, fire is spreading in every direction, and we must flee! I'll take you to our country villa, then return to Rome and help to stamp out the fire and stop the pillaging. Hurry, while the Appian Way remains clear!"

While shouting these awful words, Marcus was unharnessing Hamilcar Barca from the chariot and harnessing him instead to a cart large enough to hold everybody. But where were Miranda and Punka?

"Get in!" said Marcus.

Instead, Claudia made a dash for the house to find her two cats, and her mother raced after her. "Miranda! Punka!" they called. They called sternly and they called coaxingly, but there was no answer. They were nowhere in sight. That is the way with cats...if someone wants them to come, they go, and if someone wants them to go, they come. Zag was already in the driver's place, for that is the way with dogs...they always get in the driver's place, never to be left behind.

"Miranda! Punka!" Claudia called again, and her mother whistled a special tune she had made up that Miranda almost always came to. But still, they did not answer.

Then Hamilcar Barca gave another terrified neigh. "Wuh-huh-huh-huh!" It would be impossible to hold him back another moment. "Come, Claudia! Lavinia, come!" shouted Marcus. "Else we all shall perish. I'll come back for the cats when I return to Rome."

There was nothing else to do. The smoke was growing denser. Everyone was choking and gasping. Claudia and her mother climbed into the cart, two frightened strangers joined them, Marcus leaped on, and Hamilcar Barca, swift as lightning, sped away.

Claudia stretched her arms back toward her pretty golden house. "Miranda!" she cried. "Punka! When shall I see you again? Where are you hiding?"

Two Brave Cats

In an urn—that was where Miranda and Punka were hiding! At the first "Wuh-huh-huh-huh!" of Hamilcar Barca, the two cats had dashed to an urn beside the pool, leaped in, and crouched at the bottom of it. It was a tight squeeze, but the urn was large, and they had done it before. They wanted to get as far as possible from the neighing, snorting, clomping, chomping horse.

Miranda's heart beat very fast as she listened to the fading hoofbeats of Hamilcar Barca. Then there was a complete silence. "He's gone," Miranda thought with satisfaction.

Miranda put one of her eyes to the crack in the urn and looked into the garden. Claudia was not in sight. No one was. The air was gray, yet it was not night. "Woe-woe," said Miranda. No one answered her "woe-woe." Miranda realized that she and Punka were alone. She tilted her nose up and sniffed. Even way down in the bottom of the urn, she could now smell smoke. She felt a little uneasy. Black specks and ashes flickered across her view, and some fell inside and onto her and Punka. Miranda studied the specks and ashes on her fur in astonishment. She then decided that it was time to get out of the urn. "Leap!" she said to Punka.

Punka happened to be a leaping cat, not a singer, true, but a leaping cat...Punka, the leaper. She was quite extraordinary. She could leap straight up in the air, at least seven feet high, and with no running start at all. She had been born with this ability that few cats have.

Now, without one single wiggle back and forth, with no preparation, Punka leaped straight up and out of the urn, a six-foot-high leap! Ordinarily she would have landed right straight back down from where she had started, but this time she maneuvered herself so that she landed beside the urn, on the outside. It was a spectacular and successful leap. "Wah," she said. She was scared because she was all alone. Her eyes and nose were filled with smoke. "Wah," she said again, calling desperately for her mother.

"Woe-woe," Miranda answered reassuringly. "I'm coming. I'll be with you in a minute."

Miranda was not a leaping cat. She was a great mother and a fine singer. But she was not a leaper. With new kittens about to be born, she was an even worse leaper than usual. "I'll have to topple the urn over," she decided, "and then crawl out." Without knowing it, Punka was helping. In her anxiety to get close to her mother, she was rubbing her body first on one side of the urn and then the other. And inside, Miranda put her weight first on one side of the urn and then the other. The urn began to totter. Then...over it turned, and not into the pool, thank goodness. Miranda, somewhat dizzy from the rocking, crawled out.

Miranda and Punka ran into the garden. They could not see the sky because the air was now filled with black billowing smoke. The fire was coming nearer. Sometimes a gust of wind was really hot. The wind was sweeping the fire closer and closer to Miranda and Punka. Did Miranda wish now that she had heeded Claudia's beseeching calls? Probably not. Cats do not live in the past. They waste no time in brooding, and some cats, like Miranda, really like a taste of excitement and danger.

"Follow me!" Miranda said to Punka.

Punka was not the sort of cat that likes excitement and danger. To lie on her back, to be petted and admired was what she liked. She was frozen with terror. She knew something horrendous was happening. Her mother took the time to give her a one-second bath. Punka's courage was somewhat restored by the motherly act, and Miranda's courage was replenished. But now, they had to go.

So it was that Miranda and Punka, the colossal cats of the family of Marcus Luminus, left their golden house and their pretty garden and went out into the alleyway behind. They walked and crouched together, side by side, and they made their way, sometimes swiftly, sometimes slowly, to the entrance to the alleyway, where the street led straight to the Appian Way. Miranda had often traveled this road held tightly in

Claudia's arms as the family went on vacation to their villa. And that was where, rightly, she supposed that her family had gone now with Hamilcar Barca.

Miranda felt exhilarated and full of brilliance. Her beautiful daughter beside her and her new little kittens, soon to be born, gave her a great sense of power and confidence. When smoke and cinders choked her daughter, she stopped long enough to give her a few reassuring licks. "It's your nose," she said, "that the bee stung. But you're all right. You'll be all right," she said.

"Wah," said Punka.

However, the minute that Miranda saw the street that led to the Appian Way, she knew she and Punka could not go that way and that she must think of another plan. The street was thronged with men, women, and children, with cows, horses, donkeys, dogs, and also a few cats, these last held mainly in someone's arms. Sacred geese from the Temple of Juno came cackling by. Everyone was trying to get out of Rome and wait for the fire to be put out and the barbarians routed.

Miranda viewed the throng with distaste. "Woe-woe," she said. She had not meant to cry but could not help it, for the spectacle was truly

terrifying. "Back into the alleyway!" she told
Punka. "Make a dash!" She had resolved to get
to the high wall at the other end of the alleyway,
for she thought that once she and Punka were
beyond the wall, they would be safe and that the
high wall would stop the fire. She told this plan
to Punka so that there would be no slip, like
Punka losing her wits, for example, tearing off

and having to be found. Only Miranda and a few other cats, the lizard cat from Barcelona, for one, knew of a secret way, through a little tunnel that was supposed to carry rainwater beneath this high wall.

"Wah," said Punka, who was going to stick to her mother and be safe and sound, and not lose her wits and tear off.

"We are going to make the dash through the fire and the smoke, now," Miranda said. "Come on, Punka!"

Punka could have made her famous leap clean over the fire and not have to race through it; but she did not want to leave her mother. Wiggling, preparing for the great dash, they hesitated. What had they heard?

"Mew, mew, mew!" Frantic little mew-mews from the doorway beside them. That was what they heard.

"Wait!" cried Miranda, her heart torn by the mew-mews. She looked into the doorway to see what was there.

Four! Four little, tiny, hardly-able-to-stand-up kittens. "Mew-mew! Help!" they cried.

Rescuing the Kittens

Miranda looked at the four little kittens in dismay. There was no big person nor any big mother cat minding them. They were all alone in the fire and the sacking and the smoke. They would die! It was a wonder they had not already choked from the smoke, their little mouths were so wide open in their piteous cries for help.

"Mew, mew, mew," they cried more frantically than ever, now that they sensed help was near.

"Woe-woe," said Miranda gently. But there was no time for further tenderness. She picked up one of the kittens in her mouth by the nape of its neck, beckoned to Punka to grab another, and they dashed through the thick smoke and sparks into the alleyway. They laid down those first two kittens, tore back through the smoke, grabbed up the other two, and successfully made the dash back to safety.

Then Miranda and Punka each carried one of the little kittens in her mouth and shoved the other two ahead of them, as gently as possible, farther and farther from where the thick smoke hung and toward the high ancient wall at the other end of the alleyway.

Punka had a little trouble with her kittens. Although she had had some experience with tiny kittens, having helped her mother raise her second litter, minding them and teaching them to walk and to play games, still she had never carried a kitten in her mouth before and did not have the knack. Her kitten kept slipping out of her mouth. But Miranda encouraged her daughter, told her she was doing very nicely, for what she was doing was not easy . . . to carry one kitten in her mouth and shove another along with her paws and be careful not to hurt it. Also, the loud mewing of the rolled-along kittens was very hard to endure. They kept proclaiming that they did not like this game of being rolled along like a fur ball and that they wanted their mother, their real right milk-giving mother, they were hungry. The kittens in the mouths of Miranda and Punka could not utter. But Miranda and Punka made them all take turns, now two in mouths and two rolled along, now the others. This was fair since it gave all a chance to mew and complain.

Sometimes they stopped to rest. The four little kittens would snuggle close to Miranda, and although Punka was helping to rescue them, she was jealous and tried to get between. Miranda understood her jealousy and washed Punka's face and told her that she was the best. She admonished her to set a good example and be brave, to try not to say "wah." Thus Miranda restored Punka's sense of security and also her own. So far she had successfully concealed any sense of anxiety from the others. She acted bored instead, as though she had lived through many experiences as bad as, if not worse than, this. She made up some story, and the kittens grinned.

Finally they reached the ancient wall at the end of the alleyway, and there, while Miranda formulated a plan to get them all over it, they rested again.

In the past Miranda had frequently gone to the other side of the wall by way of the little tunnel that was supposed to carry off rainwater. Once the lizard cat and Miranda had met head on inside of it. Of course the lizard cat had had to back out, for Miranda would never retreat. Now, how to get the little kittens through the dark little tunnel and not lose any of them? That was what Miranda wondered.

Then Punka, who had never before made up a plan, made one now. She told it to her mother, and her mother purred. Punka's prowess as a leaper had not gone unnoticed by Miranda. Sometimes in the garden she would watch her daughter make the unexpected high leap straight up in the air and straight down again, and she would study the feat with cool detachment. Now she listened in approval to Punka's plan, which was to leap up and over the ancient wall with a kitten in her mouth...all four of the kittens, in fact, one by one.

"All right," said Miranda, and she purred. "Go ahead."

So Punka took one of the kittens in her mouth, got a firm grip on it, not to drop it, studied the wall a second (it was more than six feet high, it was seven!) and leaped! Straight up she leaped, and down she came on the other side of the alley wall.

Miranda put her ear to the wall. "Wah," said Punka.

"Woe-woe," answered Miranda. It sounded as though she said "*Io!*"—which means "Hurrah!" in Latin.

Punka repeated the feat three times. All the kittens were now on the safe other side of the wall. Miranda took her usual route through the little tunnel, for she was not a leaping cat. And now she and Punka and the four little kittens, their heads bobbling dizzily from the aerial escapade, were reunited.

There was not as much smoke on this side of the wall and no flames, no sparks at all. They were safe. However, Miranda felt that they must find shelter soon, for night was coming. So on they pressed. The going was tedious and rough. To make matters worse, Miranda found another little abandoned baby kitten, and this one could not walk either. She and Punka now had five unable-to-walk kittens to save and to succor. Supposing the wind shifted and the fire returned to this side of the city?

"The first four must learn to walk," Miranda said to Punka. "Stand up!" she ordered them. "Stand!" she repeated when the little ones simply stared at her with their jaws hanging open stupidly. "Now!" commanded Miranda. "Like this. You walk like this."

Miranda paraded back and forth before the waifs with her head high and her tail stiff. The little ones tried, but they kept falling over. A little tiger cat who had silently and suddenly joined them laughed. Miranda cuffed him. "You may stay with us," she said, "if you are nice."

The kittens tried again and again. Pretty soon they could stand and they could walk from Miranda to Punka and from Punka to Miranda without tumbling. "Mew, mew!" they cried in exultation.

"What an achievement!" Miranda gave each one a swift little lick or two. However, now that the kittens could walk, they were harder to manage than they had been before. Being babies, they had already forgotten the terrible danger from which Miranda and Punka had just rescued them. They began to frisk about, to play punch games with each other, and even to run away.

"Stop!" commanded Miranda. "You must save your strength. Stop that this minute!"

Grinning, the four kittens careened as fast as they could away from Miranda and safety. Though exhausted, Miranda and Punka rounded them up. And it was time to go. Miranda picked up the new little sooty-colored kitten that was really too young to walk, and she led the procession. Punka had to bring up the rear, carry whatever little kitten might tire and have to be carried for a ways, keep count, make sure that all were together, and not let any of the new walkers get lost.

Miranda was very proud of the way Punka was handling things and rubbed up against her lovingly for a moment. Pampered! That is what people used to say about Punka! Look at her now! A high leaper, an important rescuer of lost cats. A princess. The Princess Punka.

"Wah!" said Punka. She wished she could

stop being brave and be pampered again, pampered, petted, and admired.

The little tiger cat turned out to be a fine assistant. He walked first on one side of the kittens and then on the other and kept the line straight. When extra kittens tried to come along, he did not say, "No. Go away!" He was an including cat, not an excluding one. Miranda purred.

Thus the procession of cats and kittens went up the street and past the Roman Forum. Some rather mean cats had taken refuge there, and they hissed menacingly at Miranda. Miranda had to put her little sooty baby down and fight off one bold cat who thought that she and her kittens had come to stay. He went and hid behind a fallen pillar because he could see that

Miranda was a miraculous, possibly dangerous cat. Shaking herself, Miranda picked up her sooty-paws again and led her group away. There were seventeen kittens now.

"We are nearly there," Miranda told them.

"Mew-mew," said the little ones, much comforted.

Where "there" was going to be, Miranda did not know herself. However, she knew she would recognize it when they reached it as the best of all possible places for herself, Punka, and all the tired, exhausted little kittens. Suddenly Miranda stopped short. They had come upon a broad and beautiful square. Miranda put down sooty-paws, and she said, "Woe-woe. Halt!"

All gladly halted. There, across the square, was a magnificent building, rounded in form, some of it battered away, but much of it still standing. It had been hurt before in other wars. Today's bombardment had hurt it still more.

This was the Colosseum! And this was where the colossal gold cat named Miranda and her colossal silver daughter cat named Punka had, by happenstance, led their troop of rescued kittens! For a moment all sat and studied this great and somewhat ruined building.

Then Miranda stood up. They all stood up.

"Woe-woe!" said Miranda. She picked up the baby kitten in her mouth, and she marched through the lofty archway where once proud chariots had rolled.

"Mew-mew," said the kittens, filing in one by one.

They knew what a triumphal procession they had made, for not a one had tumbled, and they grinned.

"There," said Miranda as she gathered her orphans into a safe and shadowy corner. "Now," she said, "we can wash ourselves." And they all did. "We are home," said Miranda. The word brought peace to the little ones and to Punka. "Take a nap," said Miranda.

But, just as they were all ready to do this, too, all curled up in tight little balls, from way down deep inside the Colosseum there came reverberating a great and awful roar.

"Urr-roorah! Urr-roorah!"

Miranda, Punka, and the kittens sat up straight. Their hair bristled; their tails puffed out. They stood on stiff legs, and then the kittens ran to Miranda in terror. What was that? That great and awful roar?

Miranda raised a paw to silence the kittens.

She glared into the gloom beyond, and she listened. There it went again . . . "Urr-rurruh-roo!"

Miranda turned to the kittens. "It is a lion," she announced calmly. "A king lion or a queen lion. Lions are always kings or queens."

"Wah," said Punka. And all the little ones opened their mouths to say "mew-mew." But no sound came out. They were hoarse from smoke, from past crying, and from present terror. These silent mews were very unsettling to Miranda, and she knew that she had to do something about the lion right away. But what?

5

The Lion

Before Miranda and the kittens took posses-sion of it, great games were held in the Colosseum for the entertainment of the em-peror and the Roman people. Sometimes these games consisted of combats between people and beasts, sometimes between just beasts. There were dens, cages, and chains beneath the floor where captive beasts and men were locked.

Miranda did not know about that custom.

But she did understand the language of the lion, for lions belong to the cat family. "Let me out of here. Oh, please someone let me out! Uh-rooruh-rurruh-ruh!" the lion said. "I think I should be let out," it said.

Miranda agreed. She and the lion wanted the same thing . . . that the lion get out, for she had decided that this place, this great big somewhat-ruined Colosseum, was going to be her place, hers and Punka's and the little rescued kittens'. A Colosseum for cats only, especially cats lost and driven about by the fates. No lions allowed.

Miranda understood that the lion was locked up, which was a comfort. But the kittens could not rest or sleep with all that noise, and she had to get him out, chase him away. While thinking how to do this, Miranda gave herself a little bath, also a few absent-minded licks to the tiny kitten who was turning out to be white. Meanwhile, the lion roared and did not let up. All the kittens turned their eyes to Miranda to see what she would do. They were not afraid any more because they knew that their rescuer, great Mother Miranda, would not let anything hurt them, but they mewed anyway, their silent mews. And Punka said, "Wah!"

Miranda stood up. She stretched. Then she said, "I am going to chase the lion away and stop all that noise. Be good little kittens and do exactly what Punka says. Hide under that nice old toga," she told the kittens. To Punka, she said, "Don't let any get lost. There are thirty-three now..."

"Thirty-four," interrupted Punka.

Miranda gave Punka a loving lick on her face. She admired the way Punka had come to her help and often on their long way here had amused and encouraged the little ones with one of her noted perpendicular leaps. She praised her.

"Wah," said Punka, proud to be part of destiny.

"Well," said Miranda. "Now to chase the lion away. We, the cats, certain good cats, of Rome, are going to live here now. I'll be back soon," she promised. "What's one lion? Don't worry. *Vale.* Farewell."

Miranda set her square little jaw and went boldly forth toward the arena. She held her head high and her tail straight up and waving like a banner. She looked splendid. "She looks like a queen," said the tiger kitten hoarsely, and all the kittens watched her until she was out of sight.

Once out of sight, Miranda raced swiftly to the shadows. She passed several corridors that led down to the area below, but so far she had not reached the right one. The lion had not roared for a while, probably being tired out. But Miranda knew she would find him, silent or not, for cats always know where another animal is.

In the quietude, as she crouched along her way, Miranda's thoughts drifted back to all the kittens. They must have something to eat. She must bring them food. What she needed most was another mother cat, a real right milk-giving mother. First...get the lion out. Then...find a nice milk-giving mother, some mother or other that had some milk...

Just then, and very nearby, the lion blasted forth with a terrible roar. "Uh-rorrah-rorrah-rorrah! Get me out! Let me out!" it said.

"How unsettling," thought Miranda as she came crouching along the side of the corridor, following the roars. She sniffed the dirt pathway. It smelled strongly of lion. She cleaned a paw and said calmly to herself, "Now the time has come to let the lion out. It is not hard to let lions out," she said bravely.

Silently Miranda approached the lion's cage. The nearer she came to it, the more nervous she

became, and often she had to stop and clean a paw or her stomach. She wondered when her new kittens would come. The thought of them and of the adopted ones, and of Punka, strengthened her. She put on a very sinister and hateful expression, and thus, in this malevolent fashion, she approached the lion's cage, sidewise.

There the lion was, prowling back and forth

inside its cage, uttering roars of anguish and despair. Miranda crouched down in front of the cage and studied the great beast. She may have been a colossal cat, but a lion is even more colossal, and Miranda was filled with awe. Then her eyes widened. Miranda had expected to see King Lion. Instead, she saw Queen Lion, Queen Mother Lion and filled with milk!

How extraordinary and how handy! No wonder the lion was roaring and bellowing and pleading to be let out. She wanted to find her cubs.

The next surprise for Miranda, who understood locks and bolts, was that the great bolt that locked the cage had loosened. Here was a lion who thought herself locked up. Yet all the while, if she could break the chain around her leg, all she had to do was push her huge paws against the bars, the door would swing open, and out she could go! Miranda felt she could easily outwit this lion. She decided that now was the time to present herself. She went boldly right up to the lion's cage, and she kept her malevolent look on her face, and she sat down in front of the cage. She let out a piercing cry. "Woe-woe!" she cried in the key of E. It sounded sinister and terrible. "Woe-woe," cried Miranda again. Up and down the scale she went, and it did sound terrible. It would scare anybody. The lion heard her, and, terrified, she gave a mighty leap.

6

A Drop of Lion's Milk

Aghast, Miranda saw that the lion's leap had broken her shackles. They had already been weakened by her desperate struggling, were old and rusty anyway, and probably dated from the days of Hadrian the Great. Although the lion could now easily get herself out of her cage, fortunately she had not taken in this fact, and she kept pacing back and forth with head bowed and her eyes on Miranda. Both the lion and the cat looked narrow-eyed and sinister and sized each other up.

Miranda thought that the lion might soon catch on to the fact that all she had to do now was open the door and go free, so Miranda had to act quickly. She wanted to strike a bargain with the lion.

"Woe-woe," said Miranda in a conversational way, not quite so sinister.

The lion stopped pacing and looked at Miranda and then said, as though asking a question, "Uh-roor-rooruh?"

This meant, could Miranda help her get out of the cage? Having put the question, she continued her pacing inside the cage, and Miranda paced outside the cage, and so the two paced and twitched their tails and watched each other with sidewise glances.

Suddenly Miranda paused. "I can get you out of the cage. I, Miranda, and only I know how to get you out. I promise to do this, but on two conditions. One, that you do not repay me for my kindness by eating me up...I have heard of lions who do this. You let a lion out, and what does he do? Thank you politely and go away to the woods? No. Eat you up, turn right around and eat you up!"

"How rough!" said the lion. "I would never do that."

Miranda paced again; the lion, too. Then Miranda stated the other condition. This was that, before the lion raced off to wherever she wanted to go, she would pause long enough to give Miranda's children some milk.

"I said," Miranda repeated, for the lion seemed astonished at the request, "do you have some milk to spare? Because I have thirty-three kittens...Punka counted thirty-four; perhaps she is including herself...and they are all crying and they need milk. I say, as one mother to another, will you let them have some? Or," and now Miranda turned around as though to leave, "must I go away and leave you here to die of thirst and hunger? And try to find some nicer lion, a more generous one, a kinder one?"

The lioness stood stock-still, and she cocked her head. Stock-still, she studied Miranda, who resumed her malevolent and sinister expression.

"You! You have thirty-three cubs!" said the lion incredulously.

"Or thirty-four," said Miranda nonchalantly, licking a paw. "Kittens, not cubs," she corrected.

"No wonder you need more milk," said the lion.

"Woe-woe," said Miranda. Then, deciding that this conversation had gone on long enough, she said, "Well, will you or won't you? Give them some milk. Otherwise, here you stay! Good-by, my friend." Miranda pretended she was leaving.

"Oh, stay! Stay!" implored the lion. "Yes, I have some spare milk, and your kittens can have all they want. I have only two cubs, and I don't even know where they are." The lion sobbed, "Uh-roora-rooh!"

"You'll find them." Miranda comforted her. "Now, come along, and remember your promises."

Miranda stood up, tugged at the bars with her front paws, working them this way and that, the door swung open, and the lion walked out. Miranda bristled her fur and made her legs as tall as possible and arched her back. She bounced up and down like a boxer. She was frightened. Would the lion remember her first promise, not to eat Miranda up? Yes, she remembered, and she did not eat Miranda up. But she was forgetting all about promise number two and was about to bolt when Miranda danced right in front of her and said, "What about the milk? Want me to put you back in the cage?"

The lion stopped short, sat back on her

haunches, and then she said, "That's right. Thirty-three or four!" she roared. "Where are they?"

"Follow me," said Miranda.

The lion willingly loped along behind Miranda to where all the little kittens were, mewing hungrily and steadily. They had recovered their voices, somewhat.

The lioness gave each one of the kittens a drop of milk. Then, not stopping to grant one more favor, not waiting for "Thank you, kind lion" (Miranda was already trying to teach the kittens manners), she tore out of the Colosseum and disappeared in the direction of the seventh hill of Rome. There she told all she met that she knew a cat who had thirty-three kittens!

"Astonishing!" said an owlet and went back to sleep.

Thus was the last lion expelled from the Colosseum. Now there were only cats there. The kittens all had little round full stomachs. A drop of lion's milk is equal to an ounce of ordinary milk and is far more strengthening. The kittens closed their eyes and went to sleep, some with a little milk still left on their tiny pink mouths.

Punka looked at her mother beseechingly. "Wah?" she asked. "When do I eat? And what?"

7

Food for All

Miranda suddenly realized that she was very hungry, too. Before she could rest and sleep, she must find food for her and for Punka. She started on a tour of the quiet Colosseum. Suddenly a look of delight spread over her bright little face. She began to drool. She smelled cooked or cooking meat.

Although Miranda felt faint at the mere smell

of food, she resolutely concentrated on the succulent smells and made her way toward them. Thus, holding her nose high in the air and sniffing delicately all the time, she came upon food, cooked food, meat smoldering still from the great fire whose flames had licked within the very walls of part of the Colosseum on that terrible day of the sacking of Rome. And this great fire had cooked the meat that was supposed to be for the beasts, the lion for one, held in captivity and awaiting their turn in the arena.

The meat was cooked to a T. It was not too black and not too rare, just right.

"Woe-woe!" said Miranda happily. "*Io!*" She smelled this piece and that daintily, for she was a fastidious, non-greedy cat. Then she broke off a piece of crisp, juicy roast pork. She could not help but purr. How good! She sampled other meats and ate contentedly and did not hurry. Although she was accustomed to having Claudia cut her meat up for her into tiny bits, still she managed to break off pieces that she could manage, and she ate them with manners and gentle purrs. She had resolved that come what may, the kittens and cats that she was going to rear in the Colosseum were going to have gentle manners and were not to be servile and crude like those of the Roman Forum.

When Miranda had eaten enough and was now strong enough for whatever might happen next, she broke off a nice juicy piece for Punka and hurried back home with it.

"Wah!" said Punka, almost swallowing the tidbit whole. More than once Miranda had to caution her to eat more slowly and prettily.

Suddenly Miranda realized that she and Punka were being watched. Three large full-grown cats, visitor cats, had arrived and were crouching at the gate. Miranda hissed. The visitors did not say, "The same to you." They raised their noses to the air and sniffed. They smiled when they smelled what it was that Punka had just eaten. They stood up and waited.

Miranda narrowed her eyes and studied the visitors. She stopped midway up the scale of her song of warning because—what luck! These three lady cats calling on her in the Colosseum were mothers.

"Ladies," said Miranda, "how good of you to call. You are welcome here because you have some milk. I will give you meat, and you must give the little ones some milk. That is fair. And you may stay here in this big house that belongs to me, Miranda, to Punka, my daughter, and to the thirty-three. Come in," she said and purred.

The three big cats came slowly in and warily watched lest there be a trap of some sort. The thirty-three kittens raised their heads and said "mew-mew," for they recognized mothers.

One mother went right up to little sooty-paws and gave him some milk. It was probably her own son. "Now," said Miranda. "You must be hungry. Follow your noses. You will find juicy drippings all the way to guide you. And Punka," she said to her daughter, "suppose you lead the way since you are the hostess." This Punka did.

When Punka and the three big cats returned, each of them had a sweet, juicy morsel for the kittens. Since most of the kittens had only baby teeth, the big cats tenderized the meat in their own mouths before dropping it into the little pink mouths of the babies. The big cats smiled as they watched the tiny ones climbing over each other to get a taste of this new food and scrunching their eyes tightly in order to savor it thoroughly. What a day it had been for the kittens! First a drop of lion's milk and now roast meat! "Not many kittens have such an opportunity," thought Miranda proudly.

Then everyone, filled with delicious food and feeling safe and sound, went to sleep. Miranda slept, too, but with one eye slightly open, guarding all, as always. In the middle of the night Miranda had her new little kittens, and there were four. When Punka saw them, she was astonished. "More kittens?" she said.

But Miranda was very proud and purred. "Yes," she said. "Your little brothers and sisters."

"Wah!" said Punka.

Miranda's only regret was that the kittens had not been born soon enough to have had a drop of lion's milk. "Still," she thought, "things are going along nicely, very nicely indeed."

A growl from outside the arcade interrupted this peaceful reverie.

"Oof!"

Miranda stole down the arcade to the entrance. There were sixteen dogs out there, and perhaps they were the same sixteen she had chased off her street after the blizzard. Well, they would have to go. They would never get into her Colosseum. She had not rescued thirty-three kittens (with Punka's help, of course), chased away a lion, and had four more in fire and smoke and sacking only to stand aside for dogs. "No, they will have to go," she thought as she watched the dogs. They were having some sort of restless consultation with their leader, a gaunt gray dog.

The only dog that Miranda liked was Zag. She really loved Zag. But she knew where Zag was. Gone with Hamilcar Barca and the family to the villa, lying at her master's feet, no doubt, asleep and snoring. Well, those days were over for Miranda.

The dogs had not yet seen Miranda where she lay crouching and awaiting the right moment to attack. Suddenly she gave a terrible and awful "woe-woe," all the way up the scale and all the way down. It echoed through the arcade and aroused the sleeping cats. Punka and the three mother cats came musically, sidewise on stiff legs, and took up their position behind Miranda. The kittens, left behind, said, "Mew, mew." The lizard cat from Barcelona with the broken tail appeared from somewhere, and that made six big cats. However, Miranda could have done all the chasing away herself, and the other cats watched her in awe as round and round in front

of the dogs she circled, singing her song of warning and rejection.

But these dogs were famished. They had smelled the meat, and they were loath to depart. Miranda had to charge the great gaunt leader dog, and she had to scratch him. At the same moment, though she had not been instructed to do this—she just had the idea herself—Punka performed her perpendicular leap. She landed on gaunt dog's back, hissed in his ear, jumped off, and he fled howling, followed by the others. Punka retired to the shadows, trembling with terror at the idea of her courageous act, and her mother said, "*Io!*"

Miranda watched the dogs dashing down the street and disappearing around the circular corner of the Colosseum, all of them, that is, except one.

One dog stayed. This dog did not flee, and this dog would not go. She flattened herself down on the ground, like a great big floppy mop, and she would not go.

Miranda settled herself down in front of the dog that would not go and studied her. Then she said gently, "Who are you, doggie? Are you Zag? Zaggie?"

8

Zag and Miranda

The big dog sighed. "Uh-huh-huh-huh-hum."
She was covered with grime and soot and
ashes. There was mud in her big shaggy paws
and floppy ears.

"I know you," said Miranda again. "You are
Zag."

The dog gave a slow, tentative wag of her tail.

"I know that you are Zaggie. In disguise,"
said Miranda, her eyes narrow and thoughtful.

How Zag had got here, instead of being safe and sound with the family, was of no interest to Miranda, and she was not astonished. Always practical, Miranda rarely looked back on the past. Instead, she dealt with each moment and what it might bring with deft realism. "You can't fool me," she said. "You are Zag."

One day last summer Marcus had had to shave off all of Zag's beautiful fur because of the heat and fleas. Even so, Miranda had recognized Zag. Punka hadn't. She had hissed at the strange-looking naked dog.

"Now, Punka," Miranda had chided her daughter. "This is Zag, our dog, Zag," and she had gone up to Zag and kissed her gently on the nose, for she could see how ashamed Zag was of her appearance and how unwilling she was to come out of the corner. She did the same thing now. She went up to Zag, who was still shaking and trembling, and she touched her nose to Zag's three times, kissing her.

Zag gave her tail another wag, and the little tuft at its end swept the ground. Then she lowered her head to Miranda, who began to wash her face. "Urr-rum," sobbed Zag, not minding the attention at all, not giving one slightest little annoyed groan. Then Zag put her great shaggy head between her huge tangled paws, lay down, and gave a profound sigh of relief.

Now Punka came sidling out of the arcade, looking for her mother. There her mother was, washing the face of some dog. Just as Punka had not recognized Zag last summer when she had been shaved, so now she did not recognize her again beneath her matted fur. "Hiss!" she said.

Miranda gave Punka a cross slap. "Don't you recognize this dog ever? Your own dog? It's Zag. Dear good roll-over dog, Zaggie. Zaggie, old Zaggie, old Zaggie, old Zag."

Ashamed of herself, Punka cautiously approached Zag and smelled her. Zag spoke crossly to her, for she had never liked Punka as much as Miranda. Punka recognized the tone. "I knew it was Zag all along," she said. She was jealous and she tried, as she always had, to get between the two.

But her mother said, "Go back and mind the kittens."

"How unfair," thought Punka. But she went. Still, she wished she were back in their other real right first home, lying in the garden there, for the sight of Zag brought back those happy long-ago days. They seemed long ago, though they had ended so suddenly only yesterday. Consider those days! Sleep, sleep on the floor or sleep in the garden, and listen as in a dream to the loving words of members of the family. "Oh, isn't she beautiful! Look at that stomach! Silver, pure silver!" Not move a muscle when someone, even big Marcus, came clomping in his huge sandals. Let him or anyone step over her, and they did.

Consider her life now! "Mind the kittens! Mind the lion that she doesn't eat you! Chase away dogs! Don't let broke-tail lizard cat on our side of the arena. Do as I say!" That was Punka's lot now. "Pshewoo!" Disgusted, Punka went back to the kittens and did not leap for them even when they said please.

Then Miranda said to Zag, for she saw that a look of peace was beginning to settle on her face, "All right, Zag. Now you must come into my house, the Colosseum. And get some sleep and have something to eat. Be careful not to step on kittens. There are thirty-seven of them, I think, counting my new four."

"Uh-huh-huh." Zag sighed. Painfully, limping quite a great deal—her feet were very sore and one had been bleeding—she stood up weakly and followed Miranda into the arcade to the little room where all the kittens were. This little room was where tickets used to be given out. It was a sweet, warm, very private little apartment, just right for Miranda, Punka, thirty-seven kittens, three visiting cats who had come to stay, and one dog, Zag.

The great and awful lizard cat from Barcelona, father of Punka and her brothers and sisters, looked in once and asked to stay. But Miranda said, "No," he must stay on the other side of the arena. Sometimes you could see his eyes over there, sometimes not. He was rather like a sentinel on the outpost. "I'll nickname him 'Splendorio,' if he does a good job," Miranda mused.

Once settled on the old toga, Zag relaxed a little. Miranda went to get her a piece of meat, hoping that the lizard cat, who had discovered the supply, had not eaten it all up. He hadn't, and Miranda came back with a nice big chunk, the kind that in the old days Zag would have swallowed in a glad gulp.

But Zag did not eat the meat. She shook her head and pretended to sleep. However, when in the distance footsteps echoed from outside the Colosseum, she would sit up and listen intently.

Then she would lie down and sigh, for the foot-steps did not belong to Marcus.

Some people had begun to return to the city. The barbarians had left; the fires were mostly out. Miranda kissed Zag again. "Woe-woe," she said. "Marcus will find you. I will take care of you. Go to sleep now." Then Miranda sang a

little lullaby to the kittens, and with her little ones beside her she purred. "Purr-purr," answered the little ones. Like the gentle lapping of small waves along the beach, the kittens purred.

But Zag could not help but sob. Even in her sleep she sometimes sobbed. You would think to hear her, she was saying the name Marcus.

Reunion

Now it was seven days later. Smoke still hung heavily over some parts of the city, and sometimes in the nighttime the cats could see an old fire smoldering. But the worst was over, and for more and more people life was beginning to resume its old pattern. This was not so for the cats or for Zag. The cats had explored most of the Colosseum. Some of it was in rubble, and many of its mighty columns had fallen. But the cats liked this and thought it a splendid place to live. Zag did not think so.

Often Zag lay at the entrance to their arcade, facing the square outside, and sometimes she moaned. She rarely ate anything and merely moistened her mouth from time to time at the fountain near the gate. Miranda sometimes joined Zag, crouched beside her, and silently tried to comfort the grieving dog. Sometimes Miranda's eyes grew sad, too, as she recalled the life they once had led, gone she was sure forever. When any man came walking along, Zag would stand up, give a hopeful wag, smell the man's heels, then lie down again and heave a deep sigh.

Few of the cats remembered much about their old life, although occasionally one would wander away, perhaps trying to find its real right home again. But most would come back in the nighttime and sing. Hearing the singing, more and more cats asked to join the chorus and take up residence. Nice cats were allowed to. Sometimes, before she had begun to feel so badly, Zag would join in the nighttime singing. She would sound a bugle-like howl at exactly the right moment, and many thought it sounded excellent.

But for some days Zag had not joined in, and Miranda was worried about her. Right now Zag was lying beside Miranda in the golden glow of the late afternoon sun. All Rome looked golden, and Miranda, who was still quite sooty, had a look of antique gold. Miranda, squinting in the sunshine, watched Zag with narrowed eyes.

"The Colosseum is no place for Zag," thought Miranda. "See how thin she is getting. Her bones are beginning to stick out."

When Miranda was not watching, some cats teased Zag, particularly the brave little tiger cat who was too young to know he must feel sympathy. So Miranda resolved to take Zag back to their old home in the hope it was still there and that someone, a servant, anyone, might have returned.

Miranda told Punka her plan, and Punka wanted to go, too. "No," said Miranda. "You must be in charge here while I am away. Guard it well, for it is our house now."

"Wah," said Punka dolefully.

"I'll try to bring something good back to eat, a little fish perhaps."

"Wah," said Punka a little more cheerfully.

"Come on, Zag," said Miranda. "We're going to take a walk. We're going home."

Zag did not move. She lay on her side, panting heavily. Miranda touched her nose to Zag's. Dry, dusty, and hot...very bad signs. And Zag could not get up. Miranda said, "Woe-woe! Marcus, Zaggie, Marcus!"

Zag raised her head a little but lay back down again, prone. "I must get help," thought Miranda. "Or Zag will die of a broken heart. Punka," she said, "Zag is too weak to go. Take good care of her. I'll hurry back. But I must get help."

Miranda gave Punka and Zag swift licks on their faces, took a last look at her little kittens, saw that they were all right, said good-by, and left. She turned only once. It is hard to leave your kittens even for an errand as important as this. "By," she said. "Woe-woe."

Zag followed Miranda with her reddened sad eyes but otherwise did not move. And Punka wistfully said, "Wah!" She did not want to be in charge. "Wah!" she said again. She had wanted to go with her mother, and she would not leap when the kittens asked her to. They could never get enough of her sudden leaps and always said "mew-mew-mew" in delight and grinned. Instead, Punka watched her mother until the brave little figure disappeared from sight across the square. Miranda may have been a colossal cat, but even she looked small on the broad and bright *piazza*.

There wasn't a braver cat in the whole world, probably, than Miranda. Yet, as she made her way through the ruins and rubble, where tiny shoots of flowers and little weeds were already beginning to grow, she felt frightened. She was recalling the day of the terrible fire, and she almost wished she had not come. She hurried past the Forum, not liking the sound of the cats who had taken up residence there. She knew that now she was very near her old home... if it had not been destroyed.

At last she came to her street. Somewhat confused because many of the houses were in ruins and she had to steer around fallen columns, she stood stock-still to get her bearings. Suddenly she perked up her ears and a smile came over her face. She heard Lavinia whistling.

Lavinia was whistling the special tune she had made up that always persuaded Miranda to come in or go out when all other inducements failed. Crouching beside a chunk of marble, Miranda listened. Then, unable as always to resist the special and compelling tune, she approached

the house. Lavinia was standing in the doorway
with Claudia on one side of her and Marcus on
the other. The beautiful golden house was prac-
tically unhurt. The three had apparently just
come home, and baskets with fruit and belong-
ings were beside them. They had not yet caught
sight of Miranda.

"Woe-woe! " said Miranda plaintively.

"I heard her! I heard her!" screamed Claudia,
jumping up and down. "Miranda! Miranda!
Where are you?"

Miranda polished a paw to make sure she was tidy. Then she walked majestically out of the shadows, and purring loudly and vibrantly, she presented herself to the family.

Claudia scooped her up in her arms and smothered her with kisses. Miranda gravely returned them with her moist little nose. "Miranda! Darling Miranda! I missed you so! I didn't know what had happened to you!"

"That dirty cat is not Miranda," said Marcus.

Claudia was indignant. "Of course it's Miranda," she said. "It's dear, beautiful, golden Miranda. I recognize her 'woe-woe.'"

Miranda narrowed her eyes and coldly surveyed Marcus. What did he think? That she could keep herself spotless with forty, or however many there were now, kittens to keep clean, to teach them manners besides, and how to walk and eat, and to get them lion's milk also? Let Marcus try to do all that himself sometime. And besides all that, she had had four brand-new kittens! She would shine again. Just wait! She eyed Marcus malevolently.

"You are right," said Marcus. "This is Miranda all right. I can tell from her expression."

"And she has had her kittens!" put in Lavinia.

"Dear, darling Miranda! You have had your kittens...and where are they?"

"And Punka?" said Claudia. "Where is Punka? And Zag?" she said. "You couldn't possibly know where Zag is, could you?"

"Yes, Zag!" shouted Marcus. Marcus spoke to Miranda as though she were a foreign cat, not a Roman. "Miranda!" he shouted. "Where's Zag? Z A G, Zag. Zaggie? After all," he said to Lavinia, "if we have found Miranda, perhaps we may find that dear noble great dog, Zag. Alas! I should have tied her that day when we reached the villa. I might have known that she would try to follow me." Marcus put his face in his hands to hide his sorrow.

"We should all have thought of tying her," said Lavinia. "But we were so tired, so confused..." and Lavinia began to cry, too.

Claudia put her face in Miranda's sooty fur and sobbed. "Punka?" she said softly to Miranda. "Zag? Dear roll-over Zag? Do you know where they are, Miranda? Oh, Miranda, do you?"

Miranda looked gravely into Claudia's eyes. Then suddenly she wiggled herself free, jumped down, and ran out the gate. Stopping for a moment, giving a slight nod as though to say, "Follow me," she trotted up the street.

"She's running away!" cried Claudia. "Miranda, come back! Come back!"

Miranda paused, turned her head, and now definitely beckoned them to follow. Then she went on slowly, looking back now and then to make sure they were following. "Wirra-wirra," she said.

"Do you hear that?" said Claudia in excitement. "She wants us to follow her. That's what she did and said when her second litter of kittens was born. They were in an urn, and she kept saying, 'Wirra-wirra,' and beckoning me to go and see. Oh, what a great cat! Come on, everybody!"

So Claudia, Lavinia, and Marcus hurried after Miranda, who was now running and jumping expertly over the rubble. "What senseless destruction!" groaned Marcus. "'*O tempora! O mores!*'" he said, for he was a learned man. And when they reached the Colosseum and saw the new damage to it, again he groaned. "Ts!" he said. "Our glorious Colosseum!"

At the main entrance into the Colosseum, Miranda paused dramatically. She turned around to make sure the family was still there and then, imperiously, gave another beckoning nod. Next, with head held high and tail waving like a banner, she marched proudly through the archway. Claudia, Lavinia, and Marcus followed her in, and at the end of the arcade, in full view of the vast arena, they saw an astonishing spectacle. Even Miranda was astonished, for she had never seen this sight before either.

There, at the end of the arcade, was a pyramid of kittens! One large cat, silvery-looking, stood in front of the pyramid, which wobbled a little. Of course this was Punka, for she gave one of her matchless perpendicular leaps, straight up in the air and then straight down again, said "wah!" in her rasping, husky voice, and down came the kittens, dissolving the pyramid.

"*Io!*" said the big cats. "*Io!* Hurrah!" They said it over and over, and Miranda said "woe-woe!" which sounded much the same, ran to Punka to congratulate her, and bestowed a kiss.

Punka purred. Punka, having been born a trick cat, had, in her mother's absence and to keep all occupied and out of mischief, trained the kittens to do this remarkable feat.

Recovering from her surprise, Claudia said, "Why, that's Punka! The way she leaps! Punka, come here!"

Punka came. She rubbed herself against Claudia's legs. "Wah!" she said, and gave giant purrs. Everything Punka did was on the big scale, and her feet were truly colossal! But then, she was a colossal cat, as was her mother, Miranda.

Now this spectacle that Punka had presented for the entertainment of cats and, as it happened, humans, too, had temporarily distracted all from thoughts of Zag. But a low moan from deep in the shadows made the family turn to see what that was. They could barely make out a huge, rather formless lump. It looked like an old mop or a fur mantle, and Miranda had sat down beside it. She was crouching there silently, as though wondering when anyone would wake up to the fact that this was no old mop or fur mantle, it was...

"Zag!" cried Marcus. "Zag! Zaggie!"

The great hulk moved. Trembling, shaking, it was trying to get to its feet.

"Zaggie! Zaggie! It is Zag!" Claudia and Miranda added their words of encouragement.

"*Puella! Cara puella!* Dear girl!" That was what Marcus often called Zag, and Zag liked it.

At the sound of the beloved voice, Zag managed to hoist herself all the way up, and, weak and exhausted though she was, she leaped into the outstretched arms of her master. She put her great shaggy paws around his shoulders and slobbered his face with kisses and spoke many words. "Uh-ruh-ruh-ruh-rum!" she said.

"There, there, Zaggie!" Marcus said. "You're all right now, all right." He let Zaggie lick his face, beard and all, for as long as Zaggie wanted. This might have been forever if Lavinia had not said, "Well, now. We ought to go. Aren't we the lucky people to have found all our pets, all three of our pets?"

"And that's the way the story ends," said Claudia merrily and happily.

But that was not the end, for Miranda would not go. Instead, she beckoned to Claudia again. "Wirra-wirra," she said. And Claudia followed her into a little side room, the ticket room. Four very tiny little kittens were making sounds, the faintest of mew-mews. They were much too small for playing the pyramid game. Miranda

ran to them, and they joyously cuddled close to her.

"Oh, look!" exclaimed Claudia in delight. "These are Miranda's own little, new little kittens! Aren't they cunning! Oh, Miranda, you great, wonderful cat. You know what you are? You are Miranda the Great!"

Miranda purred at the praise. Her little square-jawed face was upturned to Claudia. But her eyes were deep and dark and sad. It seemed as though Claudia's words, "You are Miranda the Great," were resounding in the vast arena like a giant echoing whisper... Miranda the Great... Miranda the Great...

"Well," said Marcus. "Time to be going now. Gather up the cats and kittens. Don't let any of the other cats and kittens follow us. Six is plenty."

"I know," said Claudia laughingly. "I'll carry two of the kittens."

"And I the other two," said Lavinia happily.

"And that's the way the story ends," repeated Claudia even more merrily and happily than before.

But that was not the end either.

Miranda stood up majestically. "Woe-woe," she said.

And then from out of the shadows and from back in the arena came silently the throng of kittens and cat inhabitants of the Colosseum. They crouched down behind Miranda, and they eyed first her, and then the three humans, and they waited. One kitten, the little tiger, boldly said, "Hiss!" when he looked at the people, danced sidewise up to them on stiff legs, and then danced back again.

Miranda came and stood between the cats

and her family. She faced the family and crouched in her familiar "I won't move" position. Her daughter, Punka, crouched down in an identical position beside her. They always fixed it that the tips of their tails were turned in identical curves, and this they did now.

A terrible suspicion swept into Claudia's mind. "They are telling us something," she said. "They are saying they are not going home with us. Miranda. Punka. Come on, now. We have to go now," she said softly.

"Mew, mew, mew," said all the little rescued kittens, looking plaintively at Miranda. And "Hiss!" they said to the people, some looking really wicked and some quite comical.

Miranda looked first at the cats and then at her family. Otherwise, she did not move. Her eyes were sad and melancholy, for she knew what decision she had to make, had already made. Punka remained beside her; she always did what her mother did. Miranda looked up into Claudia's face, silently conveying the news to her that here she must stay, that she could not abandon the kittens she had rescued, that she could not return home, that home now for her and her rescued kittens was the Colosseum.

"Mew, mew, mew," said all the little kittens who had understood the silent speech. "Mew, mew, mew!" they cried as loudly as they could, and this meant, "Long live Miranda the Great!"

Other big cats said, "She shall be our queen. Queen Miranda of the Colosseum." Even old broke-tail lizard came out from somewhere and salaamed before Miranda—he was trying already to curry favor—and slunk back sidewise into the shadows.

"Oh, she'll come soon, I know she will," Claudia said. "Let's wait. You know how she always likes us to wait for her? Take her time?" So she and her whole family, including Zag who was growing stronger by the minute now that Marcus had come, waited.

Miranda the Great,
Queen of the Colosseum

Nighttime came. Still, Claudia and her mother and father waited. They didn't want to go home without their two big and wonderful cats. They felt compelled to stay a little longer and a little longer. They had a feeling that something was going to happen.

When the moon came out, full and shining over the far wall of the arena, Miranda stood up, stretched, and said, "Wirra-wirra!" Then, with Punka following slightly behind, like a lady in waiting, she led the cats and the kittens, smallest ones first, in straight formation around the huge arena.

Next, Miranda mounted the dais, leaped gracefully onto the throne of emperors, and with Punka standing at her side, somewhat below on a sort of a stool, she surveyed her followers. They took their places, sopranos on one side, altos and contraltos in their rightful locations. The kittens' choir was in front. The kittens wanted to practice and uttered a few faint mews, but Miranda raised a paw, and they stopped. Total silence fell over the arena. The lizard cat stood far off in the background, high on a column silhouetted against the moon.

Miranda stood up, paused a moment, and then began to sing.

A solo.

The song that Miranda sang began with a gentle theme that told of her life of ease and plenty in the pleasant garden of Claudia, a *cara puella*, seen now over there in the background. Not a cat or kitten turned to look. Suddenly Miranda let out a high note filled with foreboding and went into the awful day of the fire and the sacking of Rome, of her (and Punka's) rescuing thirty-three lost little kittens, of coming at last here to the Colosseum, of driving out the lion, of the drops of lion's milk she had bargained for with the lion, of the arrival of her four new little kittens.

She sang of these little kittens and said they might not be as strong as the original thirty-three, having been born too late for the lion's milk, but that nevertheless they were true princes and princesses and heirs to the throne on the dais, her throne, to be occupied now and forevermore by her or her offspring, though occupied in former years by proud emperors, by Vespasian and by Titus, master builders of the Colosseum.

"*Viva! Viva!*" sang the chorus. "Long live the Queen!"

While Miranda paused for breath, she encouraged other cats to enter into the chorus, even to add a short solo of their own at the right moment and in the right key, to sing of what had transpired to them on and since the fateful day of the fire.

These cats sang in all keys of the scale and in

keys that are not on the scale, such as the key of Z, in honor of Zag. Even broke-tail cat from Barcelona, known as the lizard cat, was allowed to sing. He began his song before the last singer was finished, he was so impatient to start. At first he sang from the top of the broken column, then he leaped to the top of a ruined wall, then he came nearer and nearer to the chorus, like a player coming from behind the scenes, then to take the center of the stage. In his song he told how he had made his departure from the city of Barcelona, Spain (the way he sang it, you would think he had chosen to leave and had not been chased out by the terrible rooftop cats there), and he sang of his arrival, after much wandering hither and thither, here in the Eternal City, Rome.

Miranda, still standing on the throne, listened sharply to his song, and she narrowed her eyes. "Danger is ever imminent," she thought, for this broke-tail cat from Barcelona might be plotting to seize the throne. He might be singing his plot in Spanish and inciting some cats to join him and crown him king. Therefore, Miranda raised a majestic paw and butted in at the peak of his drama with the same sort

of high note with which she had frightened off the sixteen dogs. The lizard cat got the point. Their duet was a short one, and Miranda easily drowned him out. The lizard cat staggered away, quite spent from his tremendous solo, back to the shadows where he remained for the rest of the opera.

In her next solo Miranda warned the cats and kittens that they were to live in peace and harmony here, and practice their music, and not to fall into the quarrelsome ways of the cats who were already making a bad name for themselves in the Forum, wrangling all the time. And "Let the lizard cat beware," she sang, "else he be outcast from this Colosseum as he had been from Barcelona and have to resume his wanderings."

For variety, other large cats sang their songs, some fierce, some sad and poignant, but all blended together into one splendid choir, all these individual histories being mingled and intermingled into a great magnificent rising and falling of voices such as one had never heard before. "Wah!" was the one note that Punka was allowed to sing. She sang it during an important pause, and it sounded fine but made her rather nervous, lest she sound it too soon or too late.

Miranda then entered into her third solo, which was one of tender sweetness. In it she promised that she would never leave them, never part from them, that she was their mother, their queen mother, queen cat of the Colosseum, that the kittens must have no fear, be brave as little lions, be brave as she, and lead gentle lives.

"Mew, mew, mew," sang the little kittens' choir in their sweet high voices. One, instead of singing, grinned foolishly. But Miranda did not rebuke him (it was the little tiger cat), though the others were appalled at his disrespect.

The moon shone high over the Colosseum now, and pale stars appeared as Miranda reached her last solo, singing the most tragic part of her role in the opera, singing of her decision, just made, to renounce her life of peace and plenty with Claudia and instead take up the hard, albeit regal and splendid, life here, of caring for the cats of the Colosseum and keeping it safe for them.

She turned her head toward Claudia as she sang, "Farewell, farewell, *carissima,* most dear, Claudia, farewell!" The other cats, made musical and sad by the tragedy being enacted before their very eyes, took up the theme of her farewell song and blended it into a touching chorus that, in nights to come, they would polish and refine, add to and enhance. And finally, in a great burst of lyric beauty Miranda ended the opera with a whispered "woe-woe!"

Then came the cries and howls of acclaim. "*Io! Io!*" cried some. "Bravo!" cried others. "Long live Miranda! Long live Miranda the Great! *Viva! Viva! Viva Miranda Regina!* Long live Miranda the Queen!"

It was awesome, and Claudia and her mother and father were awed. They were also sad, for they realized that the gist of all this great epic was that Miranda and Punka were not going to come home with them. Claudia stretched out her arms. "Miranda, come on. Come on," she implored.

But Miranda shook her head and said, "Woe-oh-woe!" And Punka said, "Wah."

Tears streamed down Claudia's cheeks. She flung her arms around Zag. "Well, anyway, we still have you, Zaggie. We did find you."

"We really found them all," Lavinia said gently. "And Miranda loves you as she always has. But she has adopted all these kittens, promised to be a mother to them, and you know what a good mother she has always been, a marvelous mother. She can't go back on her word."

"I know," said Claudia sadly.

They prepared to leave. It is very hard, when you have finally found your two lost cats that you have raised from kittenhood, to go away and leave them again. Marcus picked up Zaggie, big though she was, not to lose her again. "You weigh a bit more now than you did when I brought you under my tunic from Spain, eh, Zag?" he said.

Silence had descended upon the arena as they turned to leave. Suddenly Miranda came bounding up. She had some tiny thing in her mouth, its little hind legs all scrunched up, its mouth drawn back in a funny little grin. She placed the kitten at Claudia's feet. Then she turned and shot like a comet back into her adopted domain, the domain of the cats of the Colosseum of whom she was queen.

Claudia picked up the little kitten. It was golden, too, just like Miranda, all gold, a miniature Miranda. "It's one of her own new little kittens," Claudia said. "I'll name you *Parva* Miranda, little Miranda, after your mother."

Claudia ran back to thank Miranda. There she lay in the little ticket room with her other three kittens cuddled beside her. Some little orphan kittens were trying to get some milk, too, and Punka made them line up. It was remarkable how well Punka managed kittens. She had a real gift.

Miranda looked up at Claudia proudly. Her eyes were deep dark pools, wise and knowing. Claudia stooped down and kissed her on her head. "Sweet Miranda. Brave Miranda," she said. "You are great, Miranda, you are Miranda the Great, aren't you? You want to come with me, don't you? But you can't, because you have to be the mother for all these kittens, and queen besides. But I'll take good care of this little one that you gave me. I'll feed her little drops of goat's milk from a leaf of a mulberry tree, the way I used to feed you when you were little. Remember?"

A tear rolled down Claudia's cheek and fell on Miranda. "But we'll come back and visit you, bring you a little fish, enough for all, something special that you always loved...we will...yes, we'll come back and say '*Ave!* Hello!'"

"But now," said Lavinia, "it is time to say '*Vale.*'"

"*Vale*, Miranda," said Claudia. And then she was struck with a really happy thought. "Maybe, some day, when these little kittens, your own and the rescued ones, are a little bigger, maybe you will come home and say '*Ave*' to us, pay us a little visit? Maybe you will even stay a little while, will you, Miranda?"

It seemed to Claudia that Miranda smiled and nodded her head, as though she were saying, "Why, yes, I might."

Claudia and her mother and her father, with

Zag held in his arms, a huge armful, started to leave. Claudia made her kitten wave to Miranda. "She knows she could come with us, she and Punka. She wants to, but she just can't." Claudia was still trying to convince herself that this was what Miranda and Punka truly wanted. Before departing, the family turned for one last look at the majestic Colosseum.

There it stood and would stand like this, probably forever. By the light of the moon in some of the broken-down places, they could see the silhouette of a cat. A faint south wind wafted the sound of muted music to them, a rising and falling, crescendos and low moaning tones as of a multitude of cats. Were they really hearing this? Or was it the remembered music? Whether they heard it now or not did not matter. They had heard it and would never forget.

"*Vale,* Miranda," they said. "*Vale.*"

Did Miranda come back home again, ever? The way Claudia hoped she might? She did. She did exactly what Claudia had thought and hoped for. After several weeks had passed, she appeared one morning at the garden gate. The Princess Punka was at her side. Miranda had

named the broke-tail lizard cat her prime min-
ister, for he had improved his ways, and she
now called him Splendorio. When she took a
little holiday, as today, he was in charge, and
she felt that she could trust the reformed cat.
She and Punka enjoyed the petting, the good
food that Claudia gave them, and then they
took a little nap in the garden.

"And so the story had really a happy ending,
after all, didn't it, Mother?" Claudia said that
evening at dusk as they watched the two colossal gold and silver cats and the little golden kitten lolling under the mulberry tree.

"Yes," said her mother. "It did."

Miranda heard the words. She narrowed her

eyes, and she looked in her remote and queenly way from Claudia to Lavinia, then rose, stretched, said "woe-woe," and suddenly bolted out of the garden gate to make it to the Colosseum in time for her solo in the great cat cantata entitled "Song of Miranda," about to begin. She had not missed one single performance yet.

"Wah!" said Punka, and she leaped over the garden wall to join her mother, for she had never missed one either.

"Curtain time," said Claudia, laughing happily. "Curtain time for Miranda the Great! *Io!*"

EPILOGUE

Should you ever journey down the Appian Way, or some other way, to Rome and should you visit the Colosseum there, going in the nighttime and, if possible, by horse and buggy with a cloppa-cloppa over the cobble-stones, you may hear the singing there, the singing of the songs of the founding of the dynasty of cats there, the great cantata added to, changed, and embellished from night to night, but the heroic theme always the same, all praising the great and miraculous Queen of the Colosseum, Miranda. Miranda the Great. That is the song that you will hear sung there in the Colosseum, for it has come down through the ages. And perhaps you will say at the right time, in the right places, "*Io! Io!* Hurrah!"

ELEANOR ESTES (1906–1988) grew up in West Haven, Connecticut, which she renamed Cranbury for her classic stories about the Moffat and Pye families. A children's librarian for many years, she launched her writing career with the publication of *The Moffats* in 1941. Two of her outstanding books about the Moffats—*Rufus M.* and *The Middle Moffat*—were awarded Newbery Honors, as was her short novel *The Hundred Dresses.* She won the Newbery Medal for *Ginger Pye* in 1952.